FOX ALL WEEK

by Edward Marshall
pictures by James Marshall

DIAL BOOKS FOR YOUNG READERS • New York

Dial easy-to-read

To Judith Blum

Published by
Dial Books for Young Readers
2 Park Avenue
New York, New York 10016

Text copyright © 1984 by Edward Marshall
Pictures copyright © 1984 by James Marshall
All rights reserved.
Printed in Hong Kong by South China Printing Co.

The Dial Easy-to-Read logo is a trademark of
Dial Books for Young Readers,
A division of New American Library ® TM 1, 162,718

Library of Congress Cataloging in Publication Data
Marshall, Edward. Fox all week.
Summary: Fox and his friends have a different
adventure every day of the week.
[1. Friendship—Fiction. 2. Foxes—Fiction.]
I. Marshall, James, 1942–ill. II. Title. III. Series.
PZ7.M35655Fr 1984 [E] 84-1708

COBE
First Hardcover Printing 1984
ISBN 0-8037-0062-8 (tr.)
ISBN 0-8037-0066-0 (lib. bdg.)
2 4 6 8 10 9 7 5 3 1

First Trade Paperback Printing 1987
ISBN 0-8037-0008-3 (ppr.)
2 4 6 8 10 9 7 5 3 1

The art for each picture consists of an ink, pencil,
and watercolor painting, which is color-separated
and reproduced in full color.

Reading Level 2.0

MONDAY MORNING

On Monday morning

Fox was up in a flash.

"Hot dog!" he cried.

"Today Miss Moon's class

is going on a big field trip!

We'll have lots of fun!"

But when Fox looked outside,

he could not believe his eyes.

It was raining cats and dogs.

"Rats!" said Fox.

"This isn't funny."

The rain came down harder.

"School won't be any fun today,"

said Fox.

At breakfast Fox was very quiet.

"I have a sore throat," he said.

"But I will go to school anyway."

"Oh, no," said Mom.

"You will go straight to bed."

"If you say so," said Fox.

7

Fox got all nice and cozy.

He read his comic books.

He listened to the radio.

And he got lots of attention.

Outside it was still raining.

"I did the right thing," said Fox.

"Feeling any better?"
said Mom.

"Oh, no," said Fox.

"I feel much worse."

"Poor thing," said Mom.

Just then Fox heard voices.

It was Miss Moon and the class.
"We are off on our field trip!"
called out Carmen.
"A little rain can't stop us!"
said Miss Moon.

"This isn't funny," said Fox.

TUESDAY'S LUNCH

Tuesday was sunny and hot.

"You may eat lunch outside,"

said Miss Moon.

"Let's go!" cried the class.

And they all went outside.

Fox, Carmen, and Dexter sat down
and opened their lunches.

"Ugh!" said Carmen. "Tuna fish!"

"Ugh!" said Fox. "Tuna fish!"

"Oh, no!" said Dexter. "Tuna fish!"

"Let's throw our lunches away,"
said Fox.

"Let's do!" said the others.

They were so proud of themselves.

"This will teach Mom,"
said Dexter.

But soon they were very hungry.
"Whose idea was this anyway?"
said Fox.

"Guess!" said his friends.
After school they ran to look
for their sandwiches.

15

On the other side of the wall

they met a poor old cat.

"I'm so happy," said the old cat.

"A nice lunch fell from the sky!"

"Three tuna sandwiches?" said Fox.

"Gosh," said the old cat.

"Kids are really smart these days."

WEDNESDAY EVENING AT THE LIBRARY

"I like books that make me cry,"
said Carmen.

"I like books that give me
the creeps," said Dexter.

"I like books that make me laugh,"
said Fox.

"This is the funniest book
I've ever read."

And he laughed out loud.

"Control yourself!" said Carmen.

"Here comes Miss Pencil!"

"Now see here, Fox!"
said Miss Pencil.

But Fox couldn't stop laughing.
"That does it!" said Miss Pencil.
"You will have to leave.
And take your friends with you!"

"Fox got us into trouble,"
said Dexter.

"I couldn't help it," said Fox.
Suddenly they heard laughing.
They peeked in the
library window.

It was Miss Pencil.

She was reading Fox's book

and laughing herself silly.

"She's rolling around on the floor,"

said Dexter.

"Miss Pencil is strange," said Carmen.

THURSDAY
AFTER
SCHOOL

On Thursday Dexter found

a box of cigars on the sidewalk.

"I smoke cigars all the time,"

said Fox.

"You *do?*" said his friends.

"Mom doesn't care," said Fox.

"She *doesn't*?" said his friends.

"Let's smoke now," said Fox.

"Why not?" said his friends.

And they went someplace quiet.

Soon they were as sick as dogs.

"I didn't know it would be
like *this*!" said Fox.
"What!" cried Carmen.
"You said you smoke all the time!"

"I told a fib," said Fox.

"Really, Fox!" said Carmen.

"That makes me hopping mad!"

"I won't do it again," said Fox.

In an hour they felt better.

But Dexter kept on smoking.
"It makes me look smart,"
he said.

"Really, Dexter!" said his friends.

THE
FRIDAY
DINNER

Fox's mom was not
a good cook.
"Rats!" said Mom.
"I've done it again!"
"Never fear,
Fox is here,"
said Fox.
"*I* will cook dinner."

"Oh, goody!" said Mom.

"Uh-oh," said Louise.

"I must be left alone,"
said Fox.

"Come, Louise," said Mom.

Mom and Louise sat down.

They waited a long time.

They heard terrible noises.

CRASH! BANG! SMASH! SPLAT!

Finally dinner was ready.

"Fox," said Mom,

"these peanut butter and jelly

sandwiches are simply delicious."

THE
SATURDAY
VISIT

"Fox, dear!" called Mom.

"Maybe she won't see me," said Fox.

"Yoo-hoo! Fox!" called Mom.

"I won't make a sound," said Fox.

But suddenly he had to—

"AH-CHOO!"

"Ah-ha!" cried Mom.

"I was doing homework," said Fox.

"Hmmm," said Mom.

"You will have to do it later.
You and Louise must visit Grannie.
It's her birthday."

"Good old Grannie Fox," said Fox.

"Put on a white shirt and tie," said Mom.

"But it's Saturday!" cried Fox.

"You heard me," said Mom.

"I won't do it," said Fox.

But Mom got her way.

"There!" she said.

"You look very sweet.

Now don't forget to give Grannie

these chocolates."

"Come on, Louise," said Fox.

On the way to Grannie's house
they met a pretty fox.
"What a cute tie,"
said the pretty fox.
"I always wear ties," said Fox.

Louise gave Fox a look.

"Chocolates!" cried the pretty fox.

"They are for you," said Fox.

"How sweet!" said the pretty fox.

And she took the chocolates.

"Bye-bye!" she said.

"What have I done?" said Fox.

At Grannie's house Fox told
the truth about the chocolates.
"That's okay," said Grannie.
"I'll make us some fudge instead.
Now take off that hot tie."

"Gosh," said Fox. "Grannies are great!"

SUNDAY
EVENING

"Look," said Dexter.

"That must be a new kid in town."

"Why does she have a paper bag over her head?" said Fox.

"Maybe she isn't very pretty," said Carmen.

"Maybe she's shy," said Dexter.

"It isn't easy being a new kid," said Fox.

"True," said the others.

"Hello there!" called out Fox.

The new kid stopped.

She turned around.

And just then a big wind

blew away the paper bag.

Fox couldn't believe his eyes.

It was his friend Raisin!

"I got braces," she said softly.

"Oh, let's see!" said Carmen.

And everybody had a good look.

"Very pretty," they said.

"I'm getting braces soon,"

said Fox.

"They don't hurt," said Raisin.

Soon they all got tired of
talking about braces.
"Want to play with us?" said Fox.
"Sure!" said Raisin.

And they all played
until the bugs came out.